The Rescue Princesses

The Shimmering Stone

More amazing animal adventures!

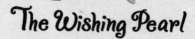

The Secret Promise

The Wishing Pearl

The Moonlight Mystery

The Stolen Crystals

The Snow Jewel

The Lost Gold

The Rescue Princesses

The Shimmering Stone

💜 **PAULA HARRISON** 💜

Scholastic Inc.

For Beatriz and Tessa, who have
the Rescue Princess spirit!

ISBN 978-0-545-50922-0

All rights reserved. Published by Scholastic Inc., 557 Broadway,
New York, NY 10012, by arrangement with Nosy Crow Ltd.

12 11 10 9 8 7 6 5 4 3 2 1   13 14 15 16 17 18/0

Printed in U.S.A.   40
First printing, December 2013

CHAPTER ONE

The Royal Wedding

Princess Amina tiptoed into the palace
courtyard and peered out from behind
a pillar, clutching her binoculars in one
hand. Her long black hair hung loosely
over her turquoise dress. On her arm
she wore a bracelet with a golden-brown
stone that shimmered as she moved.

She looked around carefully. Rows of
tables were laid out in the center of the
courtyard, ready for the banquet tonight.
There was nobody here. If she was quick,

maybe she could reach the garden without being seen! She cast one last look around before darting out of her hiding place and running across the courtyard. She'd almost reached the other side when she ran straight into her cousin Princess Rani, and tumbled to the ground.

Rani, who was much older and taller, helped her up. "Hey!" she said, laughing. "What's the hurry? Is there a wild animal chasing you?"

"Oh, sorry, Rani! I didn't see you!" gasped Amina.

"Don't worry, I'm all right!" said Rani. "But why are you in such a rush?"

"I was looking out my bedroom window with my binoculars and I'm sure I saw a tiger outside the palace wall!" explained Amina. "It was walking through the long grass next to the river. I was just going to take a closer look." She held out her binoculars. "Oh no!" She stopped and looked at them more closely.

"What's wrong?" asked Rani.

"One of the lenses is broken. I must have knocked it against the ground when I fell." She showed her cousin the crack in the glass on one side of the binoculars. Her heart sank. She used her binoculars nearly every day. They were so handy for seeing all the Kamalan wildlife.

"What a shame!" said Rani sympathetically. "I know how much you love them. Come and show me the tiger — we can close one eye and look through the side that isn't broken."

"All right, then." Amina turned toward the archway that led out to the garden.

"Rani! Amina! Where are you?" A loud voice came from inside the palace.

Amina froze. Her aunt, Queen Keshi, had been hurrying around the palace all morning. With the royal visitors due to arrive that day, there was lots to do.

"Mom wants us," said Rani. "We'll have to look for your tiger later."

"But he might be gone by then!" Amina looked longingly at the archway. If only she could get through before her aunt came along. She wanted to see the tiger so badly!

"You go, then," said Rani. "Mom probably wants me to try on my wedding dress for the hundredth time! You should go and have some fun."

Amina grinned. Even though Rani was much older, she was a perfect cousin — kind and funny. Amina was so happy that she was going to be her bridesmaid the next day!

"There you are!" Queen Keshi climbed down the steps to the courtyard, wearing a purple sari and a gold crown.

"Rani, you must try on your wedding dress one more time. Amina, I have some jobs for you to do. The royal guests are already starting to arrive and I am determined to make this the best wedding ever held in the kingdom of Kamala!"

"But, Aunt!" began Amina. "Could I go out into the garden first because —"

Queen Keshi waved her hands. "Amina! There isn't much time! We need to get the table decorations right and then we have to make sure that the guests' rooms are ready."

Amina's shoulders drooped. She wished she could go and see the tiger first. She'd seen deer and monkeys near the palace before, but never a tiger.

Rani noticed her disappointed face.

"Maybe Amina could pick some flowers from the garden to decorate the tables?" she said. "Maybe some of those pink and white lilies."

Amina perked up. If she was picking flowers in the garden, then she could sneak a look over the wall with her binoculars at the same time. She looked hopefully at her aunt.

Queen Keshi nodded. "Just make sure you pick plenty, and *don't* forget to put them in water, so that they last until the wedding. And *don't* get dirt under your fingernails!" She swept back up the steps.

Rani gave Amina a quick grin and followed her mom.

Amina hurried through the archway, grateful that Rani had found her a reason to be out in the garden. She was also glad that the queen hadn't noticed her binoculars because she would have wanted to know what Amina was up to.

She walked down to the side gate and climbed the stone steps that led up to the top of the high wall. There was a walkway there that the guards used when they were patrolling. Amina leaned her elbows on the stone and lifted the undamaged part of the binoculars to one eye.

The palace of Kamala stood on top of a hill. The countryside spread out below, full of grass and rocks and bushes. A sparkling river wound its way through the middle and purple mountains rose in the distance.

Amina scanned the tall grass near the river. At first, she couldn't see the tiger and she began to wonder if it had

disappeared among the bushes. Then a sudden movement caught her eye.

A large tiger with bold black stripes walked proudly along the riverbank and lifted its head to look around. It had a white mark on its nose.

For a moment, Amina wondered if she should have told her aunt about the tiger. Queen Keshi loved animals and had even set up a wildlife hospital on the far side of the palace grounds so that any sick animals could be cared for. But lately it had been difficult talking to her aunt because she was so busy thinking about Rani's wedding.

As Amina watched the beautiful tiger, she noticed a patch of long grass beginning to quiver. Two more animals with orange and black stripes sprang out and galloped down the river bank. These tigers were *much* smaller. They chased each other playfully and tumbled into the grass.

Amina grinned widely and her hands shook with excitement. She couldn't believe there were tiger cubs so close to the palace!

CHAPTER TWO

The Pompous Prince

The biggest tiger turned around and gave
a short growl. Instantly, the little cubs
jumped up to follow their mother. Amina
watched them for several minutes, loving
the way the cubs skipped through the
grass. She hoped she could show them
to her friends, Princesses Lottie, Isabella,
and Rosalind. They loved animals just as
much as she did, and soon they would
be arriving with their families for the
wedding!

"What are you doing?" asked a voice from below.

Amina spun around to see who it was.

A boy stood by the steps to the wall, looking up at her. *He must be one of the first wedding guests*, Amina thought.

Remembering her manners, she climbed down the steps and curtsied to him. "Hello, I'm Princess Amina! I'm Princess Rani's cousin and I live here," she told him. "Did you just arrive?"

"Yes, I'm Prince Henry from the kingdom of Guldania," he said. "I thought your palace would be a lot bigger. Ours is about ten times the size of yours!"

Amina thought this was a little rude, but maybe he didn't mean it to be. "I've just seen something amazing with my binoculars. There's a tigress and two cubs playing near the river. I can show you if you want."

"Fine, I'll look!" said Henry, snatching the binoculars from her hand.

Amina let Prince Henry climb up the wall in front of her. Even without the binoculars she could still see the tiger walking next to the river with two small fuzzy shapes bouncing along behind.

"One side of the binoculars is broken, so just look through the other side," she told him. "There they are! They're just like big stripy cats!" She pointed at the cubs.

Henry frowned darkly. "There's nothing out there that looks like a cat! I think you're making it up."

"Look!" said Amina. "They're just next to that bush by the river."

Henry thrust the binoculars back at her. "Well, I can't see them and I don't think you know anything about tigers. I don't want to use your silly binoculars anymore!" He marched down the steps.

Amina watched him go, wondering why he'd gotten so mad. She thought everyone liked watching animals. She hoped the other wedding guests would be friendlier than he was. Then she remembered that her aunt needed flowers to decorate the tables, so she hurried to pick some.

She arranged the flowers neatly and filled the vases with water before hurrying back to the wall again. Maybe her friends would arrive soon. She was sure Lottie, Isabella, and Rosalind would love seeing the tiger cubs and would agree that they were the cutest baby animals they'd ever seen!

But as the morning went on and guests from north, south, east, and west arrived, her friends still hadn't come. As she waited at the front window, Amina remembered how she'd met them a few months ago at a Royal Dance Festival.

Lottie had told them all about her older sister, Princess Emily, who had rescued animals in danger with the help of her friends.

The girls had been so excited by this idea that they promised to do the same. Then they had used their new skills to rescue a little foal. They were called the Rescue Princesses.

Amina grinned. Being a Rescue Princess was so much fun! Together they practiced running and climbing and balancing. Sometimes they used ninja moves to move around without anyone seeing them. They even had rings with magic jewels that let them call one another whenever they needed help.

She touched her sparkling emerald ring. A few weeks ago, they had rescued a baby monkey from serious danger in the depths of the tropical rain forest. It had been an adventure. It was a shame that they would be so busy with the wedding this weekend that there wouldn't be time for animal rescues.

"Come on, Amina! There's still a lot to do!" said Queen Keshi, noticing her staring out the window.

"Yes, Aunt!" said Amina.

Just then, a car pulled up outside and a princess with tight red curls climbed out.

"Lottie!" cried Amina, running outside and giving her friend a hug.

"Hello, Amina!" Lottie gave her usual grin and her green eyes sparkled. "Are the others here yet?"

"Not yet," said Amina. "But when they get here, I have something awesome to show you!"

Queen Keshi came gracefully down the steps to greet the king and queen of Middingland, Lottie's mom and dad.

Just as they were all bowing and shaking hands, two more cars pulled up with princesses inside. One princess had long, curly brown hair and wore a yellow dress. She climbed out of her car and waved at Amina and Lottie.

"Isabella! You're here at last!" cried Amina, waving back.

A girl with short blond hair climbed out of the other car with a frown on her face. "I don't see why I had to wear this long dress today," she said, twitching her blue velvet skirt. "It's too hot. It would have been better to wear shorts!"

"But, Rosalind!" said her mom weakly. "We had to arrive looking nice. This is a very important occasion!"

Amina hurried over to the blond-haired princess. "Hello, Rosalind! Would you like to come inside for a cold drink?"

Rosalind's frown lifted a little. "Yes please! I'm really thirsty. Do you have any ice cubes? I love drinks with ice cubes."

"I think so. Follow me!" Leaving the grown-ups to finish their royal greetings, Amina led her friends inside. Then she got glasses of lemonade for them with ice cubes and straws.

"So is it your sister who's getting married tomorrow?" Lottie asked Amina.

"No, Rani's my cousin," explained Amina. "My parents died of a fever when I was little, and my aunt and uncle have taken care of me ever since. Rani's much older than us, she's twenty."

"You're so lucky to be a bridesmaid," said Isabella. "Do you have a special dress?"

Amina nodded. "It's a turquoise sari, decorated with gold thread. I can't wait to show it to you!" She pushed back her long hair and the golden-brown stone on her bracelet shimmered. "I have something else to show you, too! This morning, I saw a tigress with two cubs near the riverbank. It was so exciting! I've never seen tiger cubs before."

"Let's go and look at them right now!" Lottie leapt up, her red curls bouncing.

"Yes, let's!" said Isabella. "Come on, Rosalind."

"But first we have to look for the lost *Book of Ninja*," said Rosalind.

"The lost what?" asked Isabella.

Rosalind rolled her eyes. "Don't you remember? It's the book that shows you every single ninja move that's ever been invented. No one's seen it for years. We talked about it last time we met up and you said that your palace had a huge library, Amina. Then you *promised* that you'd look for it in there."

"Oh! I do remember now!" cried Amina. "Everything's been so busy with the wedding that I completely forgot to look for it. Sorry, Rosalind!"

"Now that we're here we can all look together," said Lottie. "But let's see the tiger cubs first. I bet they're so cute!"

They all looked at Rosalind, who noisily sucked up the last drops of lemonade through her straw. "I guess it would be cool to see the tiger cubs," she said at last.

Amina beamed. "Great! I know you're going to love them!"

CHAPTER THREE

The Wildlife Hospital

Amina ran upstairs to get her binoculars from her bedroom. Then she led her friends through the courtyard into the garden and up the stone steps to the top of the wall. But just as they reached the top and looked down at the countryside below, a white van painted with a green cross came roaring out of the main palace gates. It raced down the winding road and stopped near the river. Four figures jumped out.

"What's going on?" asked Isabella, wide-eyed.

"I don't know." Amina bit her lip. "That van is the one that belongs to the wildlife hospital on the other side of the palace. They pick up injured animals and take them to the hospital to get better."

The vets opened the back doors of the van, pulled out a large white stretcher, and carried it down to the edge of the river.

"It must be a big animal to need a stretcher that size," said Rosalind.

Amina's heart began to thump. She looked through her binoculars to try to see what was going on. She hoped the tiger cubs weren't hurt.

A few moments later, the vets carried the stretcher back to the van. The animal they carried had orange and black stripes but it was much bigger than the cubs.

"I think it's a fully grown tiger," she told the other princesses. "But I can't really see it because of all the people crowding around it."

"Poor thing! I wonder how it got hurt," said Isabella. "Is that the same tigress you were talking about, Amina?"

"I'm not sure." Amina twisted her bracelet anxiously. What if it *was* the same tigress? And where were the cubs? Had they been hurt, too?

"This is awful! I have to find out what's going on!" She hung the binoculars around her neck and raced back down the steps and along the path that led to the wildlife hospital. The other girls ran after her.

The white van with the green cross drove past them and pulled up outside the redbrick hospital. The girls rushed after it, reaching the van just as the vets

climbed out. Two men and two women dressed in white coats opened the back of the van and pulled out the stretcher. Amina only caught a glimpse of the animal, but she knew right away that it was the tigress she'd seen that morning.

"It *is* the same one — she's the cubs' mother," Amina told the others. "I recognize that white mark on her nose."

The tigress made a snuffling noise and one of her paws twitched. "Dr. Patel?" Amina called to one of the vets. "Can you tell us what happened to the tigress?"

The vet turned around. "She has a broken leg. We think she was probably injured while hunting for food. We've given her an injection to help her sleep and now we'll see if we can heal her leg." She closed the van doors and then followed the stretcher inside.

"At least the cubs didn't get hurt," said Isabella.

"But this is almost as bad," Amina burst out. "The cubs are little! They're too small to survive on their own without their mother. What if they find themselves in danger?"

"You should tell the vets," suggested Rosalind. "They could look after the cubs until their mom is better."

Amina knew instantly that Rosalind was right, so she ran up to the door and knocked quickly.

A man came to the door and stared at the princesses in surprise. "Yes, what is it?"

"It's just . . ." Amina stumbled over her words. "I mean, I saw some tiger cubs out there near the river and I'm very worried about them. . . ."

"It's all right!" said the vet. "It's a fully grown tiger that's been hurt. There are no injured cubs here. Now I must go, there's a lot of work to do on the tigress's leg." He began to shut the door.

"No, that's not . . . I didn't mean that!" said Amina desperately, but before she could explain, Lottie, Isabella, and Rosalind all started talking at once.

"We have to save the cubs!" said Lottie.

"There are two sweet little tigers. . . ." added Isabella.

"This is an emergency!" snapped Rosalind.

"Princesses!" The man held up one hand, frowning. "I have to go and help the other vets." Amina's heart sank as he closed the door on them firmly.

"*Now* what do we do?" cried Isabella. "He didn't understand at all!"

"Silly man!" said Rosalind. "I hate it when people don't listen."

Lottie made a face. "There's no point in getting upset about it. We'll just have to think of something else."

"But we can't tell my aunt," said Amina anxiously. "She's so busy with all the guests arriving and she wants everything to be perfect for Rani's wedding. I don't want to ruin it all. . . ." She trailed off and stared at the ground, her stomach churning. Everything was going wrong. She didn't want to upset Queen Keshi but she *had* to help those little cubs.

"We need to hurry," insisted Rosalind. "The tiger cubs might be fine now, but what about when night comes? They need their mom to keep them safe from bigger animals."

Amina twisted her bracelet and the golden-brown stone shimmered. She glanced up and found her friends looking at her. "I think we should go and get the little cubs ourselves," she said.

"Isn't that dangerous?" asked Isabella.

"A little, but I know the countryside around here really well, so I can make sure we stay safe." Amina straightened her shoulders. "Let's go and find them right now before anyone realizes we're gone."

Lottie's green eyes sparkled. "That's a great idea, and since they're small, we'll be able to carry them back here easily. Then as soon as the tigress is better they can be together again!"

Amina nodded firmly. "It's time for another adventure!"

CHAPTER FOUR

The Fruit Sellers

The princesses walked quickly back through the palace garden.

"I love adventures!" said Isabella. "But will we be able to get out the palace gate without anyone seeing us?"

"We can use ninja moves!" said Rosalind eagerly.

"They'll have to be very good ninja moves, because there are guards watching from the palace walls all the time," said Amina.

The girls stopped near the palace gate
and looked doubtfully at the guard
standing next to it. There was no way
they could get past without him noticing.
Just then, Queen Keshi swept through the
archway and saw them. "There you are,
Princesses! It's time for you to try on your
wedding outfits to make sure that they're
perfect for tomorrow."

"But, Aunt, we were just going to . . ."
began Amina.

"Quickly now! You do want to look
nice, don't you?" said the queen. "Go and
collect your outfits from your bedrooms
and then come to the dressing room."

Reluctantly, the princesses followed
her through the courtyard and into the
palace.

"I wish we didn't have to do this," Lottie
whispered to Amina. "I want to search for
the tiger cubs right now."

They went upstairs to collect their
things. Amina left her binoculars on her
nightstand and took her bridesmaid dress
out of the wardrobe. Then she waited in
the hallway for her friends and led them
to the dressing room.

"Maybe this won't take too long," she
said hopefully. "Once my aunt leaves,
we can change really quickly and get it
over with."

But when they reached the dressing
room, Queen Keshi stayed to help them.
"I'm very good at sewing, so if your
dresses need changing, I can easily help,"
she told them. Then she fussed over them
forever, measuring their sleeves and
checking the size of each dress.

Rosalind began to glare at the queen's
tape measure, as if she was about to say
something mean.

Amina, who was worried about what

Rosalind might say, tried to think of something to get her aunt's attention. "Aunt? Did you like the flowers I picked this morning?" she asked.

"Mmm? Yes, they're very nice, thank you, dear," said Queen Keshi, looking closely at Isabella's hem.

"Will they match Rani's bouquet?" asked Amina. "I hope they don't clash."

Her aunt paused. "I hadn't thought about that! I should go and check them immediately." She laid her tape measure down on a table. "Hang up your dresses carefully when you're finished, girls!" She swept from the room.

Lottie folded her arms. "Good! Now that she's gone, we can plan what we're going to do."

"I still don't see how we're going to get out of here." Isabella pointed out the window. "That guard's still standing by

the gate and there are people looking at the view from the wall. Someone's bound to spot us."

"That's why we need ninja moves!" said Rosalind. "I *wish* we had that lost *Book of Ninja*!"

"There isn't time to look for that right now," said Lottie, causing Rosalind to glare at her.

Amina's eyes sparkled suddenly. "I know! If we look like people who are *supposed* to be walking out through the palace gate, then no one will get suspicious when they see us."

"What do you mean?" asked Isabella. "Who would be going through the gate?"

"Fruit sellers!" Amina ran to the closet in the corner and rummaged around. Then she pulled out a bundle of cotton shawls in bright pinks, greens, and yellows. "These are just like the shawls that the fruit sellers wear. They come up to the palace every day to sell their goods and then they leave again. We could disguise ourselves to look just like them!"

Lottie grabbed a green shawl, swirled it around her shoulders and then wrapped it tightly over her head so that it covered her red curls. "This is great! No one will *ever* realize it's us!"

"But we don't have any fruit," said Isabella doubtfully.

"They've usually sold everything by the time they leave," said Amina. "So we just need empty baskets and we can borrow those from the kitchen." She gave a pink shawl to Isabella and found yellow ones for herself and Rosalind.

The princesses hurriedly took off their wedding outfits and tiaras. Then they put their other clothes back on and covered themselves with the shawls as much as they could.

Isabella giggled at her reflection in the mirror. "I think this could work! I don't recognize myself at all!"

"It's a good plan," said Rosalind. "But I still think we need ninja moves, too."

"We'll definitely use some later," promised Amina. "Is everyone ready?"

But just as they were about to go, there was a knock at the door and a small princess with long blond hair walked in.

"Oh!" She stopped and looked confused. "I was told that Princess Amina would be here. Queen Keshi sent me to try on my dress. I'm Princess Samantha."

"Sorry, my dear! We're just here to sell fruit!" said Lottie in a fake croaky voice.

"I'm Princess Amina!" Amina took off her yellow shawl. "This shawl is just a disguise."

"Oh, how funny!" said Princess Samantha with a shy smile. "Are you dressing up for fun?"

Lottie and Rosalind exchanged warning looks.

Amina saw their looks but felt she should tell the truth. "Actually, we have something important to do and that's why we need them. So please don't tell anyone about it."

Princess Samantha looked solemn. "Is it important princess stuff?"

Amina nodded. "We need to save two baby animals!"

"Then I promise I won't say a word to anybody," said Samantha. "If someone comes along, I'll tell them I don't know where you are. You can trust me, I promise!"

"Thanks!" said Amina.

Princess Samantha smiled. "What kind of animals are you saving?"

"Two little tiger cubs," Amina told her. "They should be somewhere near the river. Their mother got hurt, so they're all alone."

Samantha's eyes widened. "Real tiger cubs! That's so exciting. Good luck!"

CHAPTER FIVE

The Cub Hunt

Amina led the princesses along the
winding palace hallways and down
the back stairs to the kitchen. She picked
up four empty baskets from a pile by
the door and gave three of them to the
other girls. The kitchen was full of people
rushing around and no one noticed four
princesses sneaking past.

Amina pulled her shawl tighter around
her face. "Be careful when we pass the
guards," she said. "If they look closely at

us they might realize we're not really the fruit sellers. Lottie, some of your hair is showing!"

"Oops!" said Lottie, tucking her red curls back under the shawl.

They walked through the garden, hoping that no one would stop them. Amina's heart raced as they got closer to the back gate.

The guard turned toward them. "Thank you for bringing the fruit, ladies!" he said, opening the gate. "See you again tomorrow."

"Thank you!" mumbled Amina, pulling her shawl down over her forehead.

The princesses scurried through the wooden gate and the guard closed it behind them.

"We did it!" whispered Isabella.

"Where do we go now, Amina?" asked Lottie.

"This way!" Amina took them along the stony path that led down the valley. Near the bottom, they reached a bridge that arched across the river.

"The tiger cubs were over here in the long grass," said Amina. "I'll show you."

They went along the riverbank, edging around boulders and prickly bushes.

"Is something moving over there?" said Isabella, pointing nervously at a patch of long grass.

"There is something moving — look!" Rosalind tiptoed forward.

Suddenly, a small black and orange shape sprang out of the grass and the tiger cub went bouncing toward the river, chasing after a butterfly. The butterfly got away and the cub landed on the edge of the bank, nearly toppling into the water.

"He's so small and fluffy!" said Lottie.

Amina smiled. "He's very cute!"

"Is the other cub there, too?" asked Isabella.

The girls looked at the long grass hopefully, but nothing else came out.

"Let's catch this one first and then look for the other one," said Lottie.

"Why don't I get him?" Amina put down the basket. "If we all rush at him we might scare him away." She draped the shawl over her shoulders, pushing back her long dark hair.

"See if you can get him to trust you," advised Lottie.

Amina stepped carefully along the riverbank toward the little cub. His ears pricked up and he looked at her curiously. As she came closer, he backed away, his big eyes full of fright.

Amina stood still. "Oh, don't run

away!" she whispered. "If you come with us, we'll look after you."

As she spoke, the cub's nose twitched, as if he was deciding whether or not she was dangerous. Then he opened his mouth and gave a tiny mew.

"I think he likes you!" murmured Rosalind.

Amina tiptoed a little closer.

The cub watched her carefully, but he didn't run away.

Noticing a large, smooth rock next to her, Amina sat down on it and held out her hand to the cub. He came forward and sniffed her fingers. His whiskers quivered.

"I'm Amina and these are the Rescue Princesses," said Amina gently. "We'll take care of you, I promise!"

The cub mewed a little louder. Then he licked her hand, sprang up onto her lap,

and settled down as if it was the most comfortable place in the world. Amina laughed and rubbed his warm stripy fur.

The other princesses came closer to stroke him, too.

"He's so soft!" said Isabella. "I wish we could keep him!"

"We can't keep him. He's still a wild animal," said Rosalind.

"Why don't you stay there, Amina?" said Lottie. "We'll look for the other cub."

Lottie, Isabella, and Rosalind put their baskets down next to Amina's rock. Then they crept up and down the river bank, looking into the reed patch and behind the bushes. They surprised a water bird that squawked and flew away, but there was no sign of the other cub.

Amina looked anxiously up at the palace. How long would it be before someone noticed they were gone?

She hoped they'd be able to go back through the gate without anyone getting suspicious.

She jumped as she noticed a figure standing at the top of the wall. The figure was very still. Was somebody watching them?

She shivered. What if someone had realized that they weren't really fruit sellers? After all, her friends were running up and down the riverbank, and fruit sellers didn't usually do that!

"Lottie! Isabella! Rosalind!" she called quickly. "Come back!"

The tiger cub began to wriggle in her arms as if he knew how worried she was.

"What's the matter?" asked Rosalind.

"There's someone standing at the palace wall and looking this way," said Amina. "What if they've seen us?"

Isabella drew her shawl over her brown curls. "I hope they can't tell who we are!"

"I'm sure I've seen that person before." Lottie squinted toward the figure. "I recognize her blond hair."

"Who is it?" asked Amina, her eyes wide.

"It's that princess we met just now," said Rosalind.

"Oh! You mean Princess Samantha?" said Amina.

Suddenly, the distant figure waved a long bright pink cloth over her head.

"She's got a colored shawl like the ones we're wearing," said Lottie.

"Why is she waving it?" said Isabella. "I wish she'd stop. If the kings and queens notice what she's doing, they might look over the wall and see us!"

"There must be a reason why she's doing it," said Amina. "It must be an emergency!" The tiger cub squirmed again and tried to jump off her lap.

"We should go back," said Rosalind. "We can put this cub somewhere safe and return later to find the other one."

Amina quickly scanned the riverbank. She didn't want to leave the other cub behind, but she didn't know where he was!

Up on the palace wall, Princess Samantha waved the pink shawl above her head again.

"She's definitely trying to tell us something," said Lottie. "We should go back."

"All right, then," said Amina. "But as soon as it's safe we *must* come back for the other cub."

She gently lowered the baby tiger into her basket and covered him up with her shawl. Then the princesses ran back up the path toward the palace.

Amina's heart pounded as they got closer to the gate. She hoped her aunt hadn't found out where they were. If Queen Keshi knew she was scrambling through bushes and getting dirty the day before the wedding, she would *not* be happy!

CHAPTER SIX

Hiding
Sizzle

As the princesses reached the palace
entrance, the gate swung open and
Princess Samantha stood there, clutching
the pink shawl.

"Thank goodness you came back!"
she said breathlessly. "I was worried you
wouldn't see me."

"Where's the guard?" asked Isabella.
"He was just standing here."

"I threw my hair ribbon in those bushes
and asked him to get it for me," said

Samantha. "Come inside quickly, before he comes back!"

The princesses rushed through the gate and Samantha closed it behind them. Then they scurried into the garden and hid behind a square clipped hedge.

Samantha collected her ribbon from the guard and thanked him before she came to join them. "I don't think he noticed you," she whispered.

"But why were you waving that shawl?" Rosalind asked her. "If the grown-ups had seen you, we would have been in big trouble."

"Has something happened?" asked Amina.

"It's Queen Keshi!" Samantha told her. "She's looking for all of you. She came upstairs while I was trying on my dress and now she's checking your rooms."

There was a scrabbling noise from

Amina's basket and a little black nose and a set of whiskers popped out from under the shawl.

"You did find a tiger cub!" gasped Samantha.

Amina pulled back the shawl and lovingly scratched the cub between his ears. He closed his eyes and mewed happily. "We can't let my aunt see him until we find the other cub. If she finds out where we went, she'll send the guards out to search instead of letting us go."

"But then they'll find the other cub, so at least he'll be safe," said Isabella.

"The guards would be too noisy," insisted Amina. "They'd just scare the cub away. Anyway, I don't want to ruin the wedding celebrations."

"I think we should find the other cub ourselves," agreed Lottie.

"Amina! Where are you?" Queen Keshi's voice rang out across the palace.

"That's my aunt!" Amina covered the tiger cub with her shawl again and raced through the back door of the palace.

Lottie, Isabella, and Rosalind left their empty baskets by the kitchen before they followed Amina up the stairs. Samantha came last.

Luckily, the corridor was empty. For a moment, Amina thought she heard footsteps but she couldn't see anyone.

"Did you hear something?" she asked the other princesses with a frown.

Samantha stopped and looked back around the corner. "Henry! What are you doing there?"

A boy stepped out of the shadows and Amina's heart sank as she recognized Prince Henry, the boy who had been so rude to her that morning.

"Everyone! This is my big brother, Henry," said Samantha, smiling. "Henry, come and look at this rescued tiger cub. It looks like a big cat."

Henry's face crumpled, as if he was about to cry. "I don't want to see your silly animal," he said. "Now leave me alone!" He ran away down the corridor.

Samantha put a hand to her mouth. "Oh dear! I forgot —" She broke off as Queen Keshi's piercing voice floated up the staircase. "The queen's coming! You go inside and I'll try to distract her for a moment."

"Thanks, Samantha!" Amina rushed into her bedroom, and as soon as they were all safely inside, she lifted the little cub out of the basket to give him a hug.

"You're lovely!" she told him, and he curled up in her arms and purred.

"We need to think of a name for him," said Lottie, plonking herself down next to Amina and stroking the cub.

"How about Fluffy?" said Isabella.

"That's not fierce enough for a tiger cub," replied Rosalind. "I think we should call him Wriggle, because he squirms so much!"

"What do you want to call him, Amina?" asked Lottie.

Amina gazed down at the little cub who was watching her with his big golden-brown eyes. "I'd like to call him Sizzle. I think it suits him."

The cub snuffled at her hand and then licked it with his little pink tongue.

"I think he likes that idea!" Isabella grinned.

There was a knock at the door and the princesses jumped.

"Quick! Hide all the shawls!" hissed Lottie, stuffing hers under Amina's pillow.

Rosalind and Isabella rushed to the wardrobe and threw their shawls inside.

Amina looked around, her heart pounding. Where could the little cub go?

"Amina? Are you in there?" called Queen Keshi.

"Just a minute," Amina called back. She lifted Sizzle back into the basket and kissed him on the nose. "Just be quiet, OK?" She covered him with her shawl again and then pushed the basket under her bed.

"Amina! I really do think —" began the queen.

"Sorry, Aunt!" Amina sprang to the door and opened it. "I was just cleaning up a little. Would you like me to help with the wedding flowers or the decorations?"

Queen Keshi's frown lifted. "It's nice of you to offer, but the flowers are all ready now. I just came to tell you that the evening banquet will be at six o'clock. You don't have very long to get ready." She turned to go just as Sizzle gave a low mew from underneath the bed.

"What was that?" asked Queen Keshi sharply.

Amina bit her lip. Should she say something? But if she showed her aunt the cub, she'd be interrupting all the preparations for the wedding tomorrow, and they hadn't even rescued the second cub yet.

"It was me, Your Majesty!" Lottie butted in. "It was my stomach growling. I'm just *so* hungry. I can't wait for the banquet!"

"You won't have long to wait." The queen smiled. "Hurry up and get ready now, girls." She closed the door behind her.

Amina knelt down on the floor next to her bed and gently pulled out the basket from underneath. She smiled. Sizzle was stretched out comfortably on the shawl with his eyes wide open. He twitched his nose at her and yawned.

"As soon as the banquet is over, we'll find your brother," she told him. "We won't let him stay out there all alone."

CHAPTER SEVEN

The Special Bracelet

Amina was sure that Sizzle would need some milk to drink, so she left the other princesses looking after him while she went down to the kitchen. She found an old baby bottle in a cupboard, filled it with warm milk, and took it back upstairs.

Sizzle drank hungrily from the bottle. Then, with his tummy full, he settled down for a snooze while the girls got ready for the banquet. Amina put on a dark green dress that matched her emerald ring and a tiara made from arching loops of silver. Her bracelet with its golden-brown stone gleamed brightly on her wrist.

The princesses left Sizzle sleeping and hurried downstairs to reach the dining room just in time. Amina went first. Rosalind came next, wearing a dark blue dress and a tiara decorated with sapphires. Isabella followed, wearing a long yellow dress and a swirly gold crown. Lottie came last, still trying to squash her ruby tiara on top of her red curls.

The banquet went on and on, with more and more food brought out for the royal guests. The kings and queens seemed to eat so slowly and spent so much time chatting with one another that Amina grew impatient. She wished they would hurry up so that she could rush out to look for the other tiger cub!

Prince Henry was sitting nearby and kept casting dark looks at her, but she tried to ignore him.

"I can't believe that boy over there is Samantha's brother," Lottie whispered to her. "She's so friendly but he seems awful!"

"I met him this morning before you got here," Amina whispered back. "I tried to show him the tiger cubs and I let him use my binoculars, too, but he wasn't very nice to me."

"I wonder what his problem is." Lottie caught Henry watching them again and glared back at him.

"Let's just leave him alone," whispered Amina.

As the banquet went on, Amina looked out the window and noticed that the sun was setting. She bit her lip. Why did this dinner have to take so long? The missing cub would be getting lonelier every minute and it would be almost impossible to search for him in the dark.

As soon as the last person had finished their dessert and the grown-ups were having coffee, the princesses rushed back upstairs. Sizzle was still asleep in the basket and Amina longed to pet him but she didn't want to wake him up.

"Let's change into our ninja clothes and go back to the river," said Lottie, pulling off her tiara and flinging it onto the bed.

The princesses rushed around, finding black T-shirts and dark leggings to wear. They left their tiaras on the bed, knowing that they might glimmer too much in the dark.

"Poor little cub!" said Amina. "It's going to be so hard to find him now. It's dark out there and if we use flashlights, the bright light could scare the cub away."

"But how will we find him without a flashlight?" asked Isabella.

"We'll just have to look as hard as we can," said Lottie.

"That will be pretty difficult." Rosalind folded her arms. "Tigers have good night vision. They can see in the dark, but we can't."

Amina opened her bedroom window and stared out into the darkness. The palace courtyard below was lit up but beyond the walls the countryside was black. There was no moon out tonight and she couldn't see the river at all. She went to her nightstand and picked up her binoculars. Looking through them made no difference, so she put them down again.

Sizzle woke up and mewed. Isabella picked him up and gave him some more milk. "He's so hungry!" she said.

"The other cub must be even hungrier, all alone out there."

"Let's just go!" said Lottie. "We're wasting time."

"No, wait!" Rosalind said sharply. "There has to be a better plan than just running out into the dark."

Lottie frowned at her. "Well, if you can think of one —" she began loudly.

"Shh! You'll upset Sizzle if you shout," said Isabella.

Lottie and Rosalind clamped their lips shut but glared at each other.

Amina wished they wouldn't argue. She smiled at Isabella and lifted Sizzle gently from her arms. Her bracelet with its golden-brown stone dangled from her wrist.

"I love your bracelet, Amina. What kind of jewel is that?" asked Isabella.

"It's a tiger's-eye stone," said Amina.

"It's beautiful!" said Lottie. "It really shimmers in the light."

"It's always done that," said Amina. "I think it's called a tiger's-eye stone because it looks just like a real tiger's eye!"

Just then, Sizzle stretched and yawned. "You're right! I can see a shimmering glow in Sizzle's eyes that reminds me of the stone." Isabella glanced curiously from the cub to the bracelet.

Rosalind sighed. "Yes, but it's not going to help us find the missing cub, is it?"

"Wait a minute!" Isabella said suddenly. "I remember something about tiger's-eyes in a rhyme my mom used to sing to me when I was younger:

In the dark of the night,
Use the tiger's light,
See what goes by,
Through the tiger's-eye."

"What a strange rhyme," said Lottie. "What's a tiger's light, anyway?"

"I don't know," said Isabella. "But it's about seeing in the dark, and that's what we need to do to find the other cub."

"See what goes by, through the tiger's-eye," Amina repeated, looking at her bracelet. "Tigers can see really well in the dark. So maybe this tiger's-eye stone can help us do that, too!"

"Let's see if that works!" said Isabella excitedly.

Amina put Sizzle down on the bed and undid her bracelet. Isabella took it, rushed over to the window, and held the golden-brown stone up to her eyes. "Oh! I can't see in the dark any better than before," she said, disappointed.

"I just thought of something!" said Lottie. "Remember our special rings? My sister, Emily, told me that they didn't work until they'd been shaped to bring the magic out of them." She held up her ruby ring. "Maybe we need to use the jewel-making tools to make the stone the right size and shape, too?"

"Did you bring the tools with you?" asked Rosalind.

Lottie nodded. "They're in my suitcase."

"Oh, please hurry, Lottie!" said Amina. "I want to find the poor little cub before it's too late."

CHAPTER EIGHT

The Magic Inside the Stone

Lottie ran back to her room to get the jewel-making tools.

"Do you really think this will work?" said Rosalind doubtfully. "I just don't understand how a jewel can help us see any better."

"But the rhyme says use a tiger's-eye and that's what the stone is called," said Isabella. "So there *must* be a chance that it's right."

"I hope so." Amina stroked Sizzle's tummy. Having him curled up on the bed beside her made her realize just how small and helpless the other cub would be, out there in the dark.

"Here it is!" Lottie burst in holding a large golden box. "I don't really know what all the tools do, but I'm sure we can figure it out!" She put the box down on the nightstand, moving Amina's binoculars to make room for it. Then she opened the lid.

Inside were rows of small silver tools. Amina took the tiger's-eye stone off the bracelet chain and placed it on the nightstand. Then she picked up a tiny hammer and chisel. She'd had the tiger's-eye stone for such a long time that she felt a little sad about changing it. She lifted her chin. *Finding the lost cub is more important*, she told herself.

The other princesses crowded around her. Even Sizzle pricked up his ears and watched.

"Just tap it really lightly to start with," advised Rosalind. "If you tap it too hard, then the whole thing could shatter."

Amina rested the chisel on the stone and tapped gently at one edge with the hammer. A large piece broke away, leaving the stone much smaller than before.

"Oh no! It's broken!" Isabella put her hand over her mouth.

"It's all right," said Amina, "I've got an idea." She looked carefully at the binoculars with its one broken lens. Then she chipped away the rough edges of the stone until it was completely smooth and round. Finally she picked up the binoculars, shook out the lens that had cracked that morning, and put the golden-brown stone in its place. The binoculars rested on the nightstand, with one ordinary lens and the other made of the beautiful tiger's-eye stone.

"There! It's a perfect fit!" she said.

"Awesome!" grinned Lottie. "Now we've got binoculars that let us see in the dark!"

"We don't know if they work yet," began Rosalind, but as she spoke, the tiger's-eye stone began to glow.

The glow grew brighter and brighter, until a golden shimmer rose up into the air. It hung there for a moment like a cloud of glitter, before twinkling into nothing.

"Wow! Why did it shimmer like that?" asked Isabella.

Amina lifted up the binoculars, her fingers trembling with excitement. "Maybe that was the magic starting to work!"

"Go on! Try them out!" urged Lottie.

Amina smiled. "Turn the light off first and then I'll use them." Her heart pounded as Lottie flicked off the light switch and the room went dark. She put the binoculars up to her eyes and squinted through the side that held the tiger's-eye stone. It worked! She could see everything as clearly as if it were day.

"It's fantastic!" She beamed. "Take a look!" She passed the binoculars to Lottie.

"Wow! It's so easy to see everything." Lottie stared through them before passing the binoculars to Isabella.

Isabella looked and then passed them to Rosalind, who took them and walked over to the open window.

"I can see everything out here, too!" said Rosalind excitedly. "I can even see the river."

"Then we can easily find the little cub!" said Amina, smiling.

"Finally! We can head out and use some real ninja moves," said Rosalind, flicking back her blond hair.

As they got ready to leave, Sizzle followed Amina to the door and mewed sadly at her.

Amina knelt down next to him, put her arms around his neck and rested her cheek against his soft stripy fur. "I'm sorry I have to go, Sizzle," she told him. "But we need to find your brother as soon as we can. I bet you really miss him!" She picked him up, carried him back to the basket, and put him down on top of the soft shawl. He sniffed at the binoculars that she'd hung around her neck. She stroked him a little, and he curled up and closed his eyes.

After checking that there was no one in the hallway, the princesses crept down the back stairs and past the kitchen. Voices came from the dining room.

"I bet the kings and queens are still chatting in there," whispered Lottie. "If we're lucky, the garden will be completely empty."

The girls slipped out the back door and through the garden. Orange lamps lit up the pathways, but the princesses kept to the shadows, hoping that their dark clothes made them hard to see.

As they crept past a stone fountain, they heard a rustling in the bushes.

"What was that?" whispered Amina.

They kept still, listening hard, but the sound stopped.

"It was probably just a bird," said Lottie.

They tiptoed toward the gate, until they saw a guard. They watched him walking back and forth. Then, when he turned his back, they dashed toward the gate. Amina fumbled with the bolt and pulled it open, hoping that it didn't creak. They crept through and Rosalind closed it behind them. Then they hid on the other side of the wall, trying to catch their breaths.

Out here, beyond the palace walls, it was even darker. The only light came from a scattering of stars in the night sky.

Amina lifted the binoculars to her eyes and suddenly she could see everything clearly. She could see moths fluttering in the air and a mouse scurrying through the long grass. At the bottom of the hill she could see the river, sparkling faintly in the starlight.

"You'll have to lead us down the hill, Amina," said Isabella. "I can't see a thing."

"Hold on!" Rosalind frowned. "Aren't we going to share the tiger's-eye binoculars? What was the point in all of us coming if we don't get to try them?"

"Don't argue, Rosalind!" said Lottie. "Let's just get down to the river and find the little cub."

Amina smiled at Rosalind. "You're right, we should take turns! When we reach the end of this path, you can have the binoculars."

Rosalind led the way from the path toward the river, stopping now and then to scan the landscape with the binoculars. Amina came last, listening carefully. She was sure that the lost cub would be feeling scared and alone by now, and she was determined to find him.

They climbed up onto the bridge that spanned the river. Rosalind passed the binoculars to Isabella and Lottie.

"There's something moving over there!" Lottie pointed excitedly along the riverbank. "Oh, it's just a deer."

Amina took her turn with the binoculars and she was amazed at how clear everything was using the magic tiger's-eye stone. There was the deer, walking away into the bushes. Then there was a flicker of movement just beyond.

She felt a tingle running down her neck. Was that a little paw poking out from behind a rock? Could it be the lost tiger cub?

CHAPTER NINE

Danger in the Night

"I think there's an animal over there, behind a rock," Amina told the others.

"Is it the cub?" asked Isabella.

Amina looked again. This time a small head with two furry ears poked out. "I think so!"

"Then we've found him! We can take him back to the palace and look after both the cubs together!" Lottie said triumphantly. "Phew, I was worried we'd never find him!"

Just then, the creature popped his whole head up and Amina knew from his whiskers and stripy coat that it really was the tiger cub.

"Look! You can see all of him now!" Amina handed the binoculars to Isabella and grinned. She was so relieved that finding the cub had been easier this time. But as Isabella passed the binoculars along, something made Amina glance back toward the gate.

The palace was lit up by all the orange lamps in the garden. But there was another light, too, bobbing up and down at the top of the wall. Amina stared at the small yellow circle. Was that someone with a flashlight?

"Can I borrow the binoculars?" she asked quickly. "I just saw something."

Isabella handed the binoculars back and Amina's heart sank as she looked through them. "I don't believe it! See that little light up there? That's Prince Henry standing on the top of the wall with a flashlight."

"Who cares? He'll never see us down here in the dark!" said Isabella.

"He might not see us now, but if he was in the garden when we left, then he knows we're out here somewhere," said Lottie grimly.

"Remember that rustling we heard in the bushes before we ran through the gate?" said Rosalind. "I bet that was him!"

Amina could see Prince Henry clearly through the tiger's-eye stone. He was sweeping his flashlight from side to side, as if he was searching the paths and bushes. "I'm sure he's looking for us," she told the others.

Two guards joined the prince. Amina couldn't hear them, but she could see

Henry talking and pointing to the river. Then a fourth figure, wearing a gleaming golden crown, joined them by the wall. It was Queen Keshi.

Amina gasped and dropped the binoculars. "Henry told my aunt about us! He told them all that we're out here!"

"What a tattletale!" Lottie burst out. "I'm going to find him and say exactly what I think of him when we get back to the palace!"

"Why is he being so mean?" cried Amina. "What did we ever do to upset him?" But the others couldn't answer her.

Rosalind picked up the binoculars from the ground and looked through them. "The palace gate is opening now. There are four, no, six, guards coming out and Prince Henry's with them. I guess they're coming to find us."

Men's voices drifted down the hill.

Isabella wound a lock of hair around one finger. "What should we do?"

"Can't we just show your aunt the tiger cub and explain?" said Lottie. "Won't she understand?"

Amina shook her head. "She'll be mad that we came out here by ourselves, especially because it's the night before the wedding. Anyway, the noise made by all the guards will scare the cub away before we get the chance to find him." She rushed off along the riverbank, looking for the place where she'd seen the cub. She crouched down next to a rock to find a furry face looking up at her.

"Don't be scared, little one," she whispered, holding out her hand. "We've come to help you."

The cub snuffled at her fingers for a moment. Then he backed away again.

"Amina, the guards are halfway down the hill!" said Isabella urgently. "If we don't hurry, they'll catch us."

Being as gentle as she could, Amina reached out for the cub and lifted him into her arms. She could feel his little heart pounding and she stroked his soft fur to try to calm him down.

"Can you carry him?" asked Lottie, running up to her.

"Yes, I'm all right," said Amina. "He's not heavy at all."

"Now we just need to get back inside that gate without being spotted," said Isabella with a shiver.

"I can help with that!" said Rosalind. "It's time for some ninja moves." She used the binoculars to keep track of the guards. The men came down the slope one by one with flashlights in their hands.

"This way!" hissed Rosalind, leading the girls behind a clump of reeds. "Now everyone get down!"

The princesses all ducked down as beams of light swept over their heads. Even the tiger cub seemed to know it was important to stay quiet. The men's voices and the lights moved on. Rosalind jumped up and motioned to the others.

"But there are only six of them. Where's Prince Henry?" whispered Amina.

"He's standing right next to the palace gate," said Rosalind. "We'll need a really good ninja move to get past him!"

The princesses edged closer to Prince Henry, who was pointing his light into the gloom. The closer they got, the more Amina began to worry. How were they ever going to get past him without being noticed? He must be blocking the way on purpose.

Just then Queen Keshi came striding through the gate with a large lantern. "Haven't those guards found the princesses yet? Come on, Prince Henry! Show me where they went. You're the one who saw them after all."

The princesses hardly dared to breathe. The queen stood less than ten steps from where they were hiding.

Prince Henry bowed. "I'm sorry, Your Majesty, but I hurt my ankle, so I can't go down there."

"Never mind! I'll go myself!" said Queen Keshi, marching away down the slope.

When she'd gone, Prince Henry put his hands in his pockets and whistled for a while. Then he started kicking stones down the hill as if they were soccer balls. "Goal!" he said, punching the air.

"His ankle doesn't look hurt to me," hissed Lottie. "Either he's just lazy or he wants to stay here so we can't get back through the gate."

Henry stopped suddenly and peered in their direction, as if he was listening.

Amina bit her lip. He must have heard Lottie talking. Holding the cub firmly with one arm, she picked up a stick and threw it as far as she could. It landed silently on a patch of grass.

"Why don't I try?" whispered Isabella, picking up a half-squashed fruit that was lying on the ground and throwing it.

Crash! It hit a bush farther down the path. Prince Henry swung around, shining his flashlight in that direction.

The princesses held their breath, hoping that he would follow the sound.

Prince Henry crept over to where the

fruit had landed and started searching
among the trees and bushes.

"Where are you?" he muttered. "I know
you're here!"

"Ready?" hissed Rosalind, and the
others nodded.

"Ouch!" cried Henry as he fell over and
dropped his light.

The princesses took their chance. They
slipped through the palace gate as quietly
as a night breeze. Then they ran across
the garden and raced up the back stairs,
not stopping until they'd reached the
safety of Amina's bedroom.

CHAPTER TEN

A Midnight Feast

Lottie shut the bedroom door behind them and flung herself down on a chair. "That was close! I thought Prince Henry would never move!"

"He really thought he was going to find us hiding in those bushes!" giggled Isabella.

Amina carried the tiger cub over to where Sizzle was sleeping. Sizzle woke up and yawned, showing two rows of little white teeth. At once, the other cub leapt

down from Amina's arms and skipped
over to him.

The two cubs snuffled at each other
for a moment. Then they ran all around
the room.

Amina smiled. "I think they've missed
each other."

"Let's get some milk for the new cub,"
said Isabella. "He must be hungry."

There was a soft knock at the door. "It's
only me!" said Princess Samantha. "Can I
come in? It's really important!"

"Of course you can!" Amina opened
the door.

Samantha was wearing blue pajamas,
and her blond hair hung loosely over
her shoulders. Her eyes widened as she
saw the little cubs. "Now you have two
cubs!" she cried. "They're adorable!"

"This is Sizzle and this is his brother,"
said Isabella, pointing to each cub.

"Their mother was injured and taken to the wildlife hospital," explained Amina. "We knew they wouldn't be able to survive in the wild without her."

"Wow!" Samantha looked impressed. "And your clothes are really cool!" She stared at their black tops and leggings.

"What did you want to tell us, Samantha?" asked Lottie. "You said it was something important."

"It's about Queen Keshi!" said Samantha. "My brother, Henry, told the queen that he'd seen you go out through the gate, and she checked your rooms. So she knows you haven't been in bed. They went to search for you, so I waited until I heard you coming back upstairs."

"Samantha, why *is* your brother being so mean?" asked Rosalind.

Amina bit her lip, worried that Rosalind

had been too blunt. But Samantha didn't look annoyed.

"He has been terrible today. I'm really sorry about that!" she said. "I think I know why he's being like this. You see, we have lots of animals back home in our castle and just before we left yesterday his favorite pet died. She was a big stripy ginger cat named Mrs. Tiddles and she was really old, but my brother loved her more than anything."

Amina felt a lump in her throat. She hadn't expected to feel sorry for Prince Henry after the way he'd been acting.

"I think he's still very upset about it," added Samantha.

"I don't understand why that's made him so mean," said Rosalind.

"The cubs do look a little like stripy ginger cats," said Amina. "Maybe they reminded him of his pet too much and that made him sad all over again." She smiled at Samantha. "Don't worry; I'll try to talk to him."

"But what should we do about the queen?" asked Lottie.

"Why don't you tell her you were having a midnight feast with me?" Samantha said eagerly. "She didn't look into my room at all, so she'll never know that you weren't there all the time. You could come over and have some treats now! Bring the cubs, too, if you like!"

Amina glanced through the window. The jogging beams of the flashlights seemed to be moving toward the palace again. The queen was coming back.

She couldn't help thinking that everything would have been easier if she'd told her aunt about the little cubs in the first place, but she hadn't wanted to interrupt the wedding preparations. She sighed. "All right, then. Thanks for helping us, Samantha. Let's get into pajamas and go to your room right now."

Soon the five princesses were scurrying down the hallway in pajamas. Amina carried Sizzle in her arms and Lottie carried the new cub. They hurried into Samantha's room before anyone saw them.

"We should think of a name for this cub," said Lottie, scratching the little tiger between the ears. "We can't keep calling him Sizzle's brother all the time."

"It should be something that matches Sizzle's name," said Amina, kissing Sizzle on the nose.

Samantha opened her nightstand drawer and pulled out a bag of candy. "Would you like some of these? I've got lollipops and chocolates and lemon drops, too.

Oops!" Some of the candies tumbled out through a hole in the bottom of the bag.

Lottie put down her cub to help pick them up. The little tiger chased after a lemon drop that was rolling away and pounced on it.

"There you go!" laughed Isabella. "Just call him Lemon Drop!"

"Sizzle and Lemon Drop!" said Samantha. "That really fits both of them."

There was a knock at the door.

"Amina!" said a stern voice. "Are you in there?"

Amina's heart turned cold. She'd just been bending down to pick up a fallen lollipop. She'd expected to hear her aunt coming down the hallway. They must have been giggling too much to notice.

In the middle of the silence, Sizzle let out a long mew as if he was wondering what the matter was.

Amina leapt up, grabbed both tiger cubs, and hid them under the covers. Then she sat down in front of them to hide the huge lumps sticking out of the bed. "Come in, Aunt," she called.

The door swung open and Queen Keshi's eyes swept around the room. "What on earth is going on?"

"We were just eating candy, Your Majesty," said Lottie.

"I can see that!" said Queen Keshi. "Amina, have you been in here all this time?"

Amina could feel the little cubs scrabbling around under the sheets behind her. She didn't want to lie to her aunt. It was time to stop hiding the cubs and explain. She took a deep breath, stood up, and pulled back the sheets. "We were rescuing these tiger cubs, Aunt. They were all on their own by the river after their mother was taken to the wildlife hospital."

Queen Keshi drew in her breath sharply. "You mean . . . you brought wild animals into the palace . . . while we have kings and queens visiting from all over the world? Did you even *think* about the wedding tomorrow?"

Amina's cheeks flushed. "That's why I didn't tell you about them before. I didn't want to make things harder. I was going to take them right over to the wildlife hospital to join their mom, but then we couldn't find the second cub and I knew he'd be in danger all by himself." She stopped and took a deep breath, tears coming to her eyes. "I'm really sorry I upset you." Sizzle pawed at her knee, so she picked him up and hugged him.

Queen Keshi patted her shoulder. "You were brave to find them yourselves. I

always knew you loved animals, Amina. I just didn't expect you to go on a rescue mission in the middle of an important royal occasion!"

Someone coughed and Prince Henry looked around the edge of the door. Samantha jumped up. "Henry, the mother of these tiger cubs was hurt and that's why the princesses were trying to help her cubs!"

"I know, I heard what she said just now," he looked at Amina. "I'm really sorry about everything. It was all a big mistake. . . . I was sad about my cat, you see. . . ." He broke off and sniffed.

He did look sorry, Amina thought. "It's all right," she said. "Would you like to meet Sizzle and Lemon Drop?"

Henry managed to smile a little. "Yes, please. Which one is which?"

Amina showed him the cubs and picked up Lemon Drop for him to hold.

"I'm glad that you're all making friends at last," said Queen Keshi. "Are you *sure* that these cubs belong with the tigress that was taken to the wildlife hospital?"

Amina nodded. "I saw them all together this morning."

"Excellent!" said the queen. "You should take them down there immediately. I know the tigress is getting better. She'll be happy to see her cubs again."

"You mean we can take the cubs over there now?" asked Amina.

"Of course!" said the queen. "The best place for these cubs is with their mother. You're not too tired to carry them, are you?"

"No, we're not tired!" cried Amina. "We'll take them right now!"

CHAPTER ELEVEN

The Secret Key

Amina, Isabella, Lottie, and Rosalind put long cloaks over their pajamas and carried the little tiger cubs carefully over to the wildlife hospital.

Even at night, the hospital was full of noise. Amina heard monkeys chattering and birds squawking, then the long low growl of a tigress. She rang the doorbell and a lady in a white coat answered it.

"Amina!" said Dr. Patel. "It's a little late to be . . . goodness! Are those tiger cubs?"

Amina nodded. "They belong with the tigress that was brought in here."

"Well!" Dr. Patel looked at the princesses' faces. "You've obviously had a big adventure! You'd better come in."

The tigress seemed to know right away that the cubs were nearby. She paced up and down her pen, her large ears twitching. Dr. Patel placed the little tigers carefully inside and they all stood back to watch. The tigress sniffed one cub and then the other. The cubs mewed and nestled against her tummy.

Dr. Patel made chocolate milk shakes for everyone and asked them to tell her all about how they had found the cubs. The girls explained what had happened but they left out the part about the tiger's-eye jewel and the ninja moves. Those were Rescue Princess secrets after all!

"Look how happy they are now that

they're back together!" Rosalind said, looking at the cubs as they clambered happily over their mother.

The tigress had washed the cubs thoroughly with her tongue and was now lying down with her eyes half closed.

"The tigress's leg is almost better, so the whole family will be able to return to the wild in a few days," Dr. Patel told them. "These little cubs wouldn't have survived for long out there without their mother. You did a wonderful thing by saving them."

Lottie sucked up the last of her milk shake through her straw. "Can we see all the other animals now?" she asked eagerly.

"It's very late!" Dr. Patel laughed. "Come back tomorrow after the wedding, and you can meet them all."

Princess Rani got married the next day in a beautiful red-and-gold sari. She wore a necklace of sparkling rubies and a round diamond ring on her finger. It was a lovely ceremony, followed by the most enormous feast that Amina had ever seen!

"You look fantastic!" Amina told her newly married cousin as they danced together at the reception.

Rani hugged her. "Thank you! And you were the best bridesmaid a princess could ever have!"

Then Rani's new husband came to dance with her and Amina went to find the other Rescue Princesses. She found Isabella and Lottie standing at the edge of the courtyard, whispering to each other.

"Amina!" Isabella said. "We need your help!"

"What's wrong?" Amina combed back her long dark hair with her fingers. "Aren't you enjoying the wedding?"

"It's lovely!" said Isabella. "But we can't find Rosalind. We're worried that she snuck off and she'll end up in trouble if anyone finds out."

"She's not in her room or the kitchen or the dining room," said Lottie.

"Do you think she's gone to the wildlife hospital to see the cubs?" asked Amina, who was longing to see the little tigers again herself.

"We didn't see her go." Lottie clutched her ruby tiara, which was slipping sideways off her head.

"Maybe she used ninja moves and that's why we didn't see her leave," said Isabella.

"That's it!" Amina's face lit up. "Rosalind loves ninja moves so much!

Remember how she was talking about finding *The Book of Ninja*? I think she's gone to look for it." She dashed down the corridor toward the library with the others running behind her.

The library seemed empty and all the towering bookcases made the princesses feel very small.

"Rosalind, are you in here?" called Lottie.

Rosalind's blond head popped out from around the corner of a bookcase. "Of course I'm here!" she said. "I'm looking for the lost *Book of Ninja*."

"I knew you would be!" Amina smiled.

"Did you find it?" asked Isabella.

"Not yet," said Rosalind. "But I found a list of the different books that are kept here, and it says the oldest books are on shelf number three hundred and twenty-nine."

The girls rushed to find the right shelf. The shelf numbers were small and hard to read, but at last they found it. Amina took a brown book with gold writing down from the shelf, and blew the dust off the cover.

"*The Water Birds of Kamala*," she read. "That's not the right one!"

The princesses checked every single book on the shelf but none of them said *Book of Ninja* on the cover.

"What about this space?" Isabella pointed at a gap between two books. "There's a book missing here."

Rosalind bent down to look at the empty space. "There's something underneath the shelf. . . ." She peered closer. "There's something tied under here." She fiddled with a piece of string and something fell into her hand. It was a folded piece of paper and a tarnished silver locket on a long chain.

"What a beautiful locket!" cried Amina. "Try opening it!"

Rosalind opened the locket and found a tiny key inside that was smaller than her thumbnail.

"Wow! That locket looks really old," said Isabella. "I wonder what the key is for?"

Rosalind handed the locket and the key to Amina, and unfolded the paper.

"What does it say?" demanded Lottie.

" 'I am *The Book of Ninja*. I have been moved to keep my secrets safe from those who would not use them wisely,' " read Rosalind. " 'Follow me to the land of the soaring eagle. Spend time looking and I will open my pages.' "

"There's a bird on here. Maybe that's an eagle." Isabella pointed to an engraving on the front of the locket that showed a bird with huge wings.

Rosalind sighed deeply. "But that means the book isn't here and I really thought we'd find it today."

"It's like a mystery and this is a huge clue!" cried Lottie.

"I love mysteries." Amina's eyes shone. "I wonder which country it means when it talks about an eagle."

"Look! Maybe this is the place!" Isabella opened a large book that showed pictures of bears and eagles, forests and waterfalls.

"*The land of the soaring eagle!*" repeated Rosalind. "It sounds like a great place for the next Rescue Princesses' adventure!"

Can't wait for
the Rescue Princesses' next
animal adventure?

The Silver Locket

Turn the page for
a sneak peek!

CHAPTER ONE

The Land of the Soaring Eagle

Princess Rosalind carefully raked the red and gold leaves into a large pile on the grass. Then she stopped to lean on the end of her rake and gaze up at the mountains. The cold autumn air had turned her cheeks rosy and her blond hair gleamed in the sunshine. Next to her, Princess Lottie kept raking.

Behind them was an enormous redbrick house with a beautiful clock tower on top of the roof. This was the home of Mr.

Periwinkle, the famous cookie-factory owner who had invented the greatest cookie of all time — the Chocorama Crunch. He was holding an Autumn Ball and had invited royal families from all around the world to come and stay at his home.

Rosalind was very glad to be here in the beautiful country of Taldonia. Although she wished her mom hadn't volunteered them to help out with so many gardening jobs. Raking these leaves was taking a very long time.

"Hurry up, Rosalind! There are more leaves over here," called Lottie, pointing her rake at the corner of the garden.

Rosalind stared at Lottie as if she hadn't really heard her. "I'm so glad we came here."

"Me, too!" said Lottie. "It's great being

together as Rescue Princesses again! It feels like a long time since we saw each other."

Rosalind, Amina, Lottie, and Isabella had become friends when they'd first met in the springtime. Lottie had told them all about her older sister's adventures and how she and her friends had saved animals from terrible danger. They had been so excited by this idea that they had formed their own secret club and continued the work of the Rescue Princesses.

"I'm glad we're together, too," Rosalind told Lottie. "But it's not just that! This really feels like the right place to look! I think it's because of those mountains over there."

"Right place to look for what?" Lottie went back to raking furiously, making the leaves fly up and drift down again like multicolored stars.

Rosalind frowned. "You know! The lost *Book of Ninja*! The note told us to go to the land of the soaring eagle." She dug out a piece of paper from her pocket and waved it at Lottie.

"Just imagine!" she added. "The book has every single ninja move inside it. If we can find it, we'll learn so much!"

On their last adventure at Amina's palace in the kingdom of Kamala, the princesses had found a mysterious note that told them to look for a lost book called *The Book of Ninja*. Along with the note, they had also found a beautiful necklace with a silver locket, which opened up to reveal a tiny key. Rosalind, who loved mysteries, had been wearing the locket ever since and was longing to go and look for more clues.

"Oh! You're talking about that book again." Lottie shook back her red curls.

"Listen, Rosy! I know you really want to find it, but there will be lots of other fun things to do here!"

"Finding the lost *Book of Ninja* IS fun!" said Rosalind. "And don't call me Rosy. I don't like it!"

Lottie made a face. "Sorry, Ros-a-lind. Oh, look, there are the others!"

The bell inside the clock tower on the roof gave a loud chime just as two more princesses came running across the grass.

Isabella had long brown curls and sparkling eyes. Amina's black hair hung over her shoulders and she smiled shyly at the other girls. They were each carrying an empty basket.

"Guess what!" said Isabella. "We found out something amazing! You'll never guess what it is."

"Have you found *The Book of Ninja*?" Rosalind's eyes lit up.

"No, that's not it!" said Isabella.

"Have you found an animal that needs rescuing?" asked Lottie.

"No, that's not it, either!" Isabella turned to Amina. "Should we make them guess some more or just tell them . . . ?"